my Sister is bigger than me

Kate Maryon   Lisa Stubbs

For Daisy & Layla, with all my love. x
And for my darling Freddy who brings
me so much joy. x – K.M.

For the best sisters, Lil & Sky,
and the little spider who sat on my desk
and asked to be on every page – L.S.

JONATHAN CAPE

UK | USA | Canada | Ireland | Australia
India | New Zealand | South Africa

Jonathan Cape is part of the Penguin Random House group of companies
whose addresses can be found at global.penguinrandomhouse.com.

www.penguin.co.uk   www.puffin.co.uk   www.ladybird.co.uk

Penguin
Random House
UK

First published 2017
001

Text copyright © Kate Maryon, 2017
Illustrations copyright © Lisa Stubbs, 2017
The moral right of the author and illustrator has been asserted

Printed in China
A CIP catalogue record for this book is available from the British Library

ISBN: 978-1-780-08098-7

All correspondence to:
Jonathan Cape, Penguin Random House Children's,
80 Strand, London WC2R 0RL

My sister Gracie is

bigger

than

me

because she's
nearly **six**
and I am
just **three**.

mummy

spider

Gran

TINY TIM

After our snack, I say,

"Please play with me?

I'll be the monkey and you be the tree!"

"How about this?"
she says,
"I'll be the **Mum**,

I'll **tickle**
your toes
and I'll **tickle**
your tum."

She tickly-tigs, I wriggle and clap, she says . . .

"shhh, little baby

it's time for your nap."

Naps are **SO** dull
and I'm so very
happy,

I cry like a **baby**

who needs a new nappy.

"Now come along, Ava,
sit down on this log,"
she says,

"I'll be the
Princess and
you be the frog!

Soon I might kiss you,
and if you don't wince,

you'll turn
from a **frog**
to handsome
young prince."

I hop and I croak,
Gracie glitters and swirls

and swishes her long
golden **shimmering** curls.

"Now, I am
the **queen**,"
she says,
"high on my throne

and you are the
maid, so pass
me my phone!"

I curtsey and bow and try not to **frown**
when I hunt
in the toy box

and give
her a **crown**.

If **I** were the prince
instead of the maid,
I'd be in charge
of the games
that we played.

She'd be my butler
and bring me **my** things.
Then **I** would
grow up to be king
of the kings!

"Now you're at the circus,
watching so pleased," she says,

"I'll swing up **high** on my magic trapeze."

I sit on the floor, remember to clap,

then say, "Now I'm a **dancer**,

all ballet and tap!"

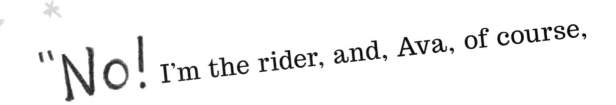

"No! I'm the rider, and, Ava, of course,

you must **giddy-up** now
because you are the horse."

"It's **my** turn to choose," I say, "I'll be a **mouse**.
You be a **hedgehog** and come to my house!"

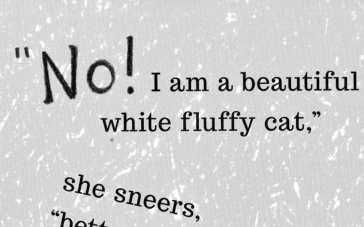

"**NO!** I am a beautiful white fluffy cat,"

she sneers, "better start running

'cause you are the **rat**."

I run away, squealing,

she **pounces** and claws

and traps me
beneath her **big**
kitty-cat paws.

"NOT playing,"

I shout,
and run to
my room

and pretend I'm a **witch**
with a cat and a broom.

I mix up a potion
and **never** will tell
if she asks me to share
my best **magical** spell.

Without even knocking, she lets herself in,
paints **green** on my lips and **hairs** on my chin.

She gets out her varnish,
says, "Ava, I might
give you long witchy nails
as **dark** as the night."

I spread out my fingers
and think I might **burst**,
I want painted nails,
but then, she says,

"First!

I'll be the doctor,
so lie on the bed,

I'll bandage you up
because you've
bashed your head."

With toilet-roll bandage she wraps round and round
and says I am too ill to make
even **one** sound.

I keep my lips zipped
but if I were the nurse
I'd make sure her bashes were
bigger and **worse**.

"Now be a crab," she says,
"or a blue whale.
I'll be a mermaid and
shimmer my tail."

I paint myself blue
and whisper a wish
and dive down so deep
that I swim with the fish.

"I am the **best**," she shouts,
"I am the **winner!**

I get to choose what
we have for our **dinner!**"

I grow a big fin. I swirl in the **dark**.
I swim to the surface, a shiny black **Shark**.

My teeth are so **big**, they're wanting to **crunch**,

but Gracie shouts . . . "Ava! I'm **not** your lunch!"

Then we giggle and laugh,
and she is a pea,

I am a dragon
and she is my tea.

I am a monster, she is the cheese,
and runs around squealing,

"Don't eat me up please!"

I am a sausage,
and she is the
mash,

so we dive in the
gravy and make
a big splash.

Then in the corner
we spy a wolf pack,
and

EeeeKKKK

we start running . . .

'cause
we are the
Snack!

At bedtime we snuggle and giggle in whispers and cuddle up close just because . . .

. . . we are sisters.